RUST & RELICS 1.5
LINDSAY BUROKER

DESTINY UNCHOSEN

Destiny Unchosen (Rust & Relics, Book 1.5)
Copyright © 2014 by Lindsay Buroker All rights reserved.
First Print Edition: January 2015

Formatting: Streetlight Graphics

No part of this book may be reproduced, scanned, or distributed in any printed or electronic form without permission. Please do not participate in or encourage piracy of copyrighted materials in violation of the author's rights. Thank you for respecting the hard work of this author.

This is a work of fiction. Names, characters, places, and incidents either are the product of the author's imagination or are used fictitiously, and any resemblance to locales, events, business establishments, or actual persons—living or dead—is entirely coincidental.

ACKNOWLEDGMENTS

Thank you to Becca Andre and Kendra Highley for reading an early copy of this story, to Shelley Holloway for editing and ebook formatting, and to Stephen Bryant (cover illustration) and Streetlight Graphics (title work and paperback formatting).

1

ONE OF THE LIGHTS FLICKERED and went out, dropping shadows on the cracked tennis court. Artemis "Temi" Sideris ignored it, swinging the racket as the machine spat another ball to her forehand. It thudded off her strings like a rifle cracking, the ball a blur as it spun over the net and landed a couple of inches from the baseline.

Temi had grown up playing on courts like this, the cool desert air whispering across her cheeks, the balls leaping in the high altitude. It reminded her of home, of her youth. If not for the constant ache in her knee—an ache that turned into a stab of pain if she rotated into her strokes the way she should—she could have pretended she was a kid again, back before she had ruined her career—her *life*—and before pointy-eared weirdos had wandered out of the mountains, telling her to trade her racket for a sword to slay monsters.

The thought, the reminder that those weirdos were supposed to come for her tonight jangled her nerves. Her belly gave a queasy lurch, and she framed the next ball, sending it over the fence and into the parking lot. Fortunately, it was Sunday night, and the dark lot was empty, devoid of witnesses.

Temi blew out a slow breath and focused on the balls

again, reciting an old poem, trying to forget the quiet terror that had been riding behind her breastbone since she agreed to this meeting.

"If you can bear to hear the truth you've spoken—" *thwack*, "—twisted by knaves to make a trap for fools—" *thwack*, "—or watch the things you gave your life to broken..."

"Kipling?"

Temi jumped a foot and almost dropped her racket. She spun toward the fence, her knee protesting the sharp movement, but she was too alarmed to grimace.

Fortunately, it was only Delia. And she was alone. No pointy-eared weirdos with her, at least not in sight.

Delia was dressed in her relic-hunting gear, wearing a bullwhip and a hunting knife in addition to jeans, a sweatshirt, and hiking boots. With her straight brown hair pulled back into a ponytail and a backpack over her shoulder, she looked ready to tramp into the woods, even if it was almost ten o'clock at night.

"Yeah, Kipling." The ball machine thunked, not spitting out any more ammo, so Temi headed for the other side of the court to turn it off.

"Not bad for a... pro athlete."

Temi had a feeling that comment had been edited mid-sentence. From high school dropout to pro athlete. "Former pro athlete," she mumbled, turning off the machine. She grabbed a hopper to pick up the balls lining the back fence, aware, as always, of the awkwardness of her gait. "I memorized it back at the academy when one of the coaches told me that a couple of the lines were above the players' entrance at Wimbledon."

"Oh, yeah? Which ones?" The gate clanged as Delia walked in and picked up a hopper to help. She glanced around, doubtlessly wondering if their new friends were indeed going to make an appearance tonight. *She* found them fascinating and would have been delighted to go off on an adventure with them. She was probably here with all of her stuff to see if she could come along.

Temi wouldn't mind the company. She still wasn't sure how much she believed about this whole situation, especially about her own blood being part... whatever. Elf, Simon said. Alien, Delia thought. Whatever the weirdos were, they weren't human. The blood sample had proven that, if their odd looks and language hadn't been clues enough.

Remembering the question, Temi said, "If you can meet with Triumph and Disaster and treat those two impostors just the same."

"So win or lose, don't go to pieces?" Delia grinned, dragging over the hopper full of balls.

"I guess. I was fifteen. The coach and I didn't spend a lot of time doing a literary analysis of the poem."

Temi rolled the ball machine into the corner and sat on a bench. Maybe the weirdos wouldn't come. Maybe they would find someone else to wield their glowing sword against the strange evil that had come to Arizona. But the special sword was tucked into her tennis bag along with her rackets, so they would at least come to retrieve it...

"You nervous about going?" Delia asked.

"Yes. Want to take my place?"

"I wish." Delia sat beside her on the bench, her olive skin contrasting with Temi's dark hands. They both might have been raised by Greek parents, but Temi still had a few memories of being an orphan in Zaire—the DR Congo now—before being adopted and brought to the United States. "But you're the one who needs..." Delia waved to Temi's knee.

The loose track pants hid the brace, but Temi never forgot it was there. "Yeah, if they can really heal it..." She swallowed. It could mean getting her career back, putting aside her mistakes and clawing her way back to the top to prove... She wasn't sure what she wanted to prove.

She couldn't fix those mistakes, couldn't bring back the people who had died while she had been driving. It was moot anyway. The weirdos wanted her to wield a sword, not a racket. "I'm just a little afraid of what they'll want in return." A lot afraid. "I'm not a warrior."

"What are you talking about? You're six feet tall and all muscle and agility and athleticism. Aside from the limp."

"I'm sure there's a mental component to thrusting swords into people."

The roar of motorcycle engines sounded in the distance. Oh God. They were coming.

"Into *monsters*," Delia said. "Monsters who kill people. Look, I know what you really want—to play tennis again. But me and Simon are going to help with the monster hunting and figure out who or what is behind making them. We'll get to the bottom of things. You won't have to do this forever."

Temi heard the Harleys approach, but didn't see them at first. The... elves—Temi couldn't keep calling them weirdos and couldn't remember the name they had used for themselves, so she had to pick something simpler—wore black leather and black helmets and weren't using their headlights. One's head turned in her direction, and she thought she spotted two violet glints. Delia had seen the elves in the dark and claimed their eyes glowed at night.

The queasy nerves returned to Temi's belly as the motorcycles pulled up in front of the courts.

"What are the odds they'll let me come along?" Delia murmured.

"I don't know."

Delia gripped Temi's arm. "Look, I'm going to try, but if they don't, learn whatever you can about the sword, will you? And about *them*. Simon and I were thinking that maybe we could figure out how to make weapons using the same technology, or maybe there are other swords like it on Earth, and then we could help you fight."

Temi looked down at her friend's hand. "Do you think it's at all strange that you're so eager to hunt man-eating monsters?"

"Yes, but technically, I think they're just man-*slaying*, not man-eating."

"Well, that's comforting then." They shared wry smiles, or maybe bemused ones, neither of them entirely understanding the other. Temi looked off to the west, to the stars in the clear sky above the dark silhouette of Thumb Butte. She didn't want to hunt anything, and, more, she didn't want to *die* hunting anything. All she wanted was her life back, another chance…

A soft clang sounded, the metal latch on the fence being lifted. The two tall, slender figures that walked in had removed their helmets, though black wool caps covered their hair. And their ears. Pointed ears. Temi and the others had seen them during that fight in the cave. Their eyes weren't glowing, not beneath the lights of the court, but they were distinct even under normal circumstances, with the younger elf, Eleriss, having deep green-blue eyes and the older one, Jakatra, having violet eyes. Temi didn't truly know if one was older than the other—neither appeared any older than her own twenty-two years, but they *seemed* older, especially Jakatra. He was more muscular than his comrade, with a hardness to his features. When Temi had first seen them, she had thought him handsome, but that had been before she learned about the ears and the eyes.

"Greetings," Eleriss said.

Jakatra said nothing, his expression flinty. The elves' facial gestures were always a little off, not quite human, but she had no trouble reading this one: he didn't want to be there. And he was the one who was supposed to teach her how to use the sword. Lovely.

Temi chose not to worry about sword training while her knee was still a question mark. Would they truly be able to heal it?

"Hey," Delia said by way of reply when Temi didn't speak. "Temi's ready. And I'm here to carry her sword for her."

Eleriss tilted his head and shared a long look with his comrade before replying. "We can only bring Artemis. Even bringing her, this is a risk. For us, for her."

"No humans allowed in the tree house, eh?" Delia asked.

"Tree... house?" Eleriss looked to the pinyon pines behind the tennis courts.

"Never mind." Delia gave Temi a long look. "This is going to be fun for you, I can tell."

"I just hope it's worth it," Temi murmured.

"Worth it, yes," Eleriss said. "A great value for you and your people. The healing and also the instruction by a talented weapons master." He pointed his palm toward his comrade.

Jakatra said something in his own language. It didn't sound flattering.

Delia leaned forward, eyes and ears intent whenever they babbled something to each other, as if she could will herself to understand them. She *did* speak several languages, but when one of her old professors had run the strangers' language sample through a computer, it hadn't matched anything in the database. The chances of picking up conversational Elf in passing were probably low.

"Temi?" Delia switched to Greek to ask a quick question that took Temi a moment to piece together. They both had Greek-speaking grandmothers and had been forced to learn some of the language as kids, but Temi had barely spoken it in the last ten years. She got the gist though: "See if you can get a dictionary for me to look at too."

Apparently Delia thought Temi would be able to go

shopping at the elf equivalent of a Barnes & Noble at some point. Temi shrugged noncommittally. She didn't truly believe the weirdos were taking her to another world. This all seemed so crazy, so far-fetched. If not for the promise that they could heal her leg, she wouldn't have agreed to any of it. Even then, she doubted they would really be able to help, not when she had seen some of the best doctors in the world already. Still, the tiniest spark of hope glowed in her mind, the hope that she was wrong.

"It would have been better to do this in *their* land," Jakatra said, switching back to English. Maybe he hadn't liked it when Delia had used a language they didn't understand. Nope, no hypocrites here.

"Yes," Eleriss said, "but they do not have strong predators like we do. Also, Master Moorisai would not come to this world."

Predators? Uh.

"Because it's forbidden. And unlike us, he pays attention to the law." Jakatra glared at his comrade again; it seemed to be his normal expression.

Eleriss only smiled benignly—that was *his* normal expression—and tilted his head toward Temi. "You are ready to depart?"

Temi took a deep breath. "Yes."

"Do not forget the sword." Jakatra pointed toward Temi's tennis bag.

The bag was zipped, the sword in its scabbard and surrounded by rackets, clothes, and boxes of protein bars. How he knew it was in there, Temi could only guess.

She picked up the bag and followed after the elves, pausing to toss Delia the keys to her car. "Don't let Simon drive it."

"I've seen *you* drive it; I don't think Simon would be tempted to go any faster or be any more reckless."

"Yes, but he'd take off on some forgotten mining road and get it stuck in a rut."

"And you don't think I would?" Delia smirked. "In pursuit of some dusty, buried antique mining equipment to sell for the business?"

Temi almost changed her mind and took the keys back, but it was a nice car. Some kids would steal it if she left it parked by the tennis courts for... however long this might take. She simply lifted a hand in farewell and walked after the elves.

"We must drive out of town before activating the portal," Eleriss said when they reached the motorcycles.

Temi adjusted the straps of her bag so she could wear it like a backpack. Jakatra already sat astride his Harley. His unfriendly expression didn't invite passengers, so Temi clambered on behind Eleriss, not wanting to grab his waist to hold on, but too busy trying to throw her knee over the seat without appearing awkward—or hurting herself—to worry about it.

When the motorcycles roared to life and charged out of the lot, Temi sent a long look back over her shoulder. Still standing on the tennis court, Delia wore a wistful expression. The unease Temi had been feeling all night returned, and she wondered if she would see her friend again.

2

THE MOTORCYCLES SLOWED TO A stop on an old logging road in the treed hills south of town. In other words, the middle of nowhere. The elves rolled the bikes off the packed dirt and parked between two trees. If the moon hadn't been out, Temi wouldn't have been able to see a thing.

"This is... the place?" she asked.

"It is suitable." Eleriss hopped off the Harley without so much as brushing her and landed lightly in the dirt.

Temi climbed off less gracefully. She supposed it was a little late to worry that she had gone off into the woods with strangers who planned to murder her and bury her body where nobody would ever find it. She had seen them fight before; it wasn't as if they would have had to take her all the way out here to kill her.

"I will camouflage the conveyance," Eleriss said, waving Temi toward the road.

Jakatra was already there, and with her first step toward him, Temi nearly tripped. Not because the earth was rough, but because his eyes were glowing faintly. She swallowed. No mistaking it this time. Eerie.

Eleriss joined them on the road, his eyes, too, glowing slightly. The motorcycles were gone. Temi stared at the spot. She had assumed camouflaging them had meant throwing some branches and leaves over them. But whatever they had done, there was no sign of the Harleys now.

Eleriss slipped his hand into the pocket of his black leather jacket. A large, rectangular blue light formed above the road a few paces away. The color and the glow reminded Temi of bioluminescent plankton she had seen on a beach in San Diego when she had been there for a tournament. But there was no water here, and the air smelled of pine and juniper, not fish and seaweed.

Without hesitating, Jakatra strode through the pale blue field and disappeared. Temi gawked. She was tempted to walk around to the other side and make sure he wasn't hiding over there somewhere. She didn't. Apparently it was time to accept that the universe was stranger than she had ever believed.

"You may go now," Eleriss said. His eyes had stopped glowing, maybe because the blue rectangle was lighting up their surroundings.

Though a dozen questions perched on the tip of Temi's tongue, she walked after Jakatra without asking them. Now that she had witnessed this promise of another world, she was impatient to see if her knee could be healed.

As she crossed through the barrier—the portal, they had called it—she met mild resistance, almost like pushing one's hand into a gelatin, but it wasn't enough to make her stop or turn around, and the sensation only lasted for a moment. Then she was standing in a very different forest, one comprised of lush greens rather than the dry dusty browns of Arizona. Sunlight filtered through a canopy of branches and leaves high overhead, the coloring off, as if she were wearing sunglasses with yellow-tinted lenses. Thick, tall trees towered all around her, rising from plants that reminded her of ferns but were much larger, more like what one might find in a jungle. A rich, loamy smell hung in air more humid than what she had left. She couldn't see any birds or animals, but heard their chirps and activities in the branches.

Eleriss stepped out of the barrier and spread his arms. "Home."

"If you say so," Temi said, though the place wasn't so exotic—so alien—as to make her feel uncomfortable. She might have believed they were still on Earth, though the strange hue of the sunlight *was* noticeable.

She spotted Jakatra ahead of them, striding along a path through the trees, already a hundred meters away. "He's not a very good guide," Temi remarked.

"He is not from this continent." Eleriss started walking, gesturing for her to come as well. "He would make a poor guide."

"So you'll be showing me around?"

"No, that is not permitted. You will be healed and trained and returned to your world as soon as possible."

"What happens if someone notices I'm here?" Temi asked. And how did she get home if these two were called away and she was left on her own?

The way Eleriss hesitated before answering wasn't inspiring. "I will have to explain the situation."

Not sure she wanted to push for more details, Temi walked after him in silence. Delia would probably be running around, taking samples of the trees and plants. Maybe Temi would bring her back a few leaves.

After fifteen minutes of walking, she and Eleriss caught up with Jakatra who was leaning against a tree next to a blanket laid over low green vegetation. He was thumbing something flat and circular in his palm. It reminded her of someone playing word games on a smartphone.

"He comes," Jakatra said without looking up.

"Good." Eleriss pointed to the blanket. "You may sit there, Artemis."

"Are we having a picnic?" Because that couldn't be what passed for an operating table here...

Eleriss did his quirky head tilt. "An... outdoor gathering in which food is consumed? Are you hungry?"

"No, I'm fine."

Temi was debating whether she wanted to explain her confusion when the elves' heads turned toward the trees behind the blanket. Between the vines dangling from the branches and the tall undergrowth covering the forest floor, it took her a moment to see what they were looking at. A figure was riding—swooping?—between the trees on a floating version of the Harleys. It had wheels and looked like a ground vehicle, but at the moment, it was gliding above the giant ferns as it veered toward them. Delia, with her interest in science fiction, would doubtlessly have a name for it, but Temi could only gape as the flying craft came to a stop near the blanket.

It settled to the ground, and its rider hopped off, a tall dark-skinned man. He was *male*, anyway; Temi wasn't sure whether these elves/aliens/whatevers could be called men and women. He wore simple green and brown clothing that flowed loosely about him, not quite hiding the easy grace he shared with Eleriss and Jakatra. Was this the healer? If so, maybe this *was* the operating room. The new elf carried a small leather bag, reminding Temi of some traveling doctor from the *Little House on the Prairie* days, though the long black hair that fell to his waist in slender elaborate braids probably wouldn't have been common in Walnut Grove.

Eleriss spoke to the new elf in his language, then handed him a small brown pouch, which quickly disappeared into a pocket with a nod. The doctor sat down cross-legged on the corner of the blanket and opened his leather bag. Temi tried to tell herself this wasn't ludicrous. A blanket in the woods... after she had been in state-of-the-art hospitals with the best doctors and medical equipment money could buy. This couldn't possibly be an improvement; God, what if it made her worse?

"He is ready for you," Eleriss said.

"Was that a payment or a bribe?" Temi asked, more to stall for time than because it mattered. She had broken out in a sweat at her last thought and groped for a way to say she had changed her mind. "Because if he doesn't want to work on humans, I'll understand." And they could go back through that portal and forget about this entire situation.

"He is a healer. He will heal anyone. The gift is to encourage his silence."

Gift. Right.

"Your kind isn't allowed here," Jakatra said bluntly, as if she hadn't figured that out yet.

"That is not entirely true," Eleriss said. "She has our blood."

"Because some randy ranger impregnated her ancestor a few centuries ago doesn't make her one of us."

Eleriss frowned at him, at Temi, then drew his comrade off, speaking rapidly in his own language.

Temi closed her eyes. She wanted to go home. As uncomfortable as home was these days, it was less strange than this place.

The doctor—healer, Eleriss had said—waved for her to approach. He had a handsome face, like the others, but it was forbidding, too, like he might be someone who would grow impatient quickly if crossed. Temi walked over, her gait more awkward than usual in the low undergrowth, and was conscious of him watching her leg. He pointed to the center of the blanket. She sat. What would she do if he pulled the equivalent of a hospital gown out of that bag and demanded she undress? Comply? Here? In the middle of the woods, with three strange guys watching her? Delia would probably punch him in the nose.

The healer pointed at her knee and said something in his language. Uh oh, did this one not speak English? Her translators were still arguing a few meters away.

Guessing at the meaning of the words, Temi pulled up the leg of her track pants. She had intentionally picked something loose enough that she could tug the hem up over her knee. He made a clucking noise. It sounded disapproving. With the exception of Eleriss's cheery words, most of the things that came out of these people's mouths did. He waved at her knee brace and said something that might have been, "Take it off."

Temi did so, though the thought that he might do something to make her injury worse came to mind again. She licked her lips, trying to see into his bag. She couldn't tell what anything was but was moderately reassured by the fact that the tools looked... gadgety. Technological rather than magical, not that she knew what "magical" instruments might look like. She just knew she would sprint back to that portal if he took out a jar of leeches.

The healer lifted her sweaty brace, gave it a sneer, and tossed it off to the side. Temi's fingers twitched toward it. She didn't want to lose it when she didn't know what the end result here would be. She could walk without it, but its support meant less pain, especially when she made sideways movements.

The healer held a palm-sized device over her knee for a minute, scrutinizing it; though if there was some readout, she couldn't see it from her angle. He poked and prodded in a couple of places. She was glad she had shaved. Next, he withdrew two brown—wooden?—disks with fuzzy undersides that reminded her of velcro. He stuck them to the skin on either side of her knee, and they remained when he removed his hands. He tapped the side of one, then sat back, looking toward Eleriss and Jakatra. They had stopped arguing and had come over to watch. Not exactly a representation of the supportive friends and family one usually had during a surgery. Of course, she hadn't had anyone supportive around during her numerous trips in and out of the hospital after the accident, either.

A faint heat emanated from the disks, warming her knee as if it were wrapped in a hot towel as part of a massage. Temi stared off into the trees. She didn't want to get her hopes up that this would do anything, yet that spark of hope kept reappearing in the back of her mind.

The healer spoke to Eleriss, who nodded and told Temi, "He believes you will be ready for full physical activity by this evening." Eleriss looked at Jakatra. "It is likely gentle training can begin." There was emphasis on the word gentle.

Jakatra said nothing. What was his reputation among his own people? Was he a jerk here too? Temi had certainly had coaches who were. Most cared, but some subscribed to that tough love method of teaching. Some resented young students with the talent to one day surpass them. At least she shouldn't have to worry about that here. The way Jakatra had moved during the fight with that monster, he would make any human look clumsy in comparison.

"Is there any chance these monsters I'm supposed to fight can be dealt with quickly?" Temi asked.

"I do not know," Eleriss said. "We have not identified who is responsible for creating them."

That would be the smart thing to do, not simply react when they showed up.

The heat had grown warmer. It wasn't painful yet, but would it become so soon? The healer was merely sitting and waiting.

"What's it doing?" Temi pointed at the disks.

Eleriss considered the question before answering. Searching for a way to say it in English? "Instructing your cells on how to heal the injury and giving them the energy to do so, so your body won't be overly drained by the process." He looked at Jakatra, as if to ask his opinion on the translation. Jakatra gave him an indifferent glance and didn't comment. "I have seen some of your scientific equipment," Eleriss said to Temi, "and it is very fascinating, but it is also very different."

"Fascinating," Jakatra said. "Right."

"Why is he helping if he hates humans so much?" Temi jerked a thumb at Jakatra, probably not as afraid of him as she should be.

"As your people would say,—" Eleriss gave his buddy another long look, "—it is a long story."

"Coercion," Jakatra said.

"Perhaps not so long a story," Eleriss said, but didn't elaborate further.

The healer removed the disks from Temi's leg. Fortunately, they peeled off without sticking to her skin. He brought back the first device, a diagnostic tool or monitor, presumably. He made a clucking noise again, this one sounding more self-congratulatory than disapproving, then returned his equipment to his bag and stood. He spoke to Temi and lifted his hand.

"You want me to get up?" She flexed her knee experimentally. It felt fine, but bending it while sitting down didn't usually hurt, so she didn't assume anything yet.

"Yes," Eleriss said. "He wishes you to stand and move before he leaves. Test it."

From habit, Temi kept her leg straight as she rose, putting most of her weight on the good one. After she was standing, she tried a knee bend. Nothing hurt. She bent deeper. Her ankle cracked, which brought an eyebrow raise from Jatakra—what, elves had perfect synovial fluid?—but the knee didn't protest the movement. She shifted her weight from side to side. Nothing.

"There is no pain?" Eleriss asked. He didn't sound surprised.

"Not at the moment." Temi felt that spark of hope growing, threatening to become a flame, but she forced herself not to assume anything yet. She could take away the pain with enough drugs, at least for a time. For all she knew, the guy had pumped morphine into her knee. But no, his gadgets hadn't broken her skin, not as far as she could tell.

"It should remain free of pain," Eleriss said. "Until Jakatra's training begins."

Coming from someone else, that might have been a joke, but Temi hadn't seen these two display much that could be considered a sense of humor.

"Then everything will be in pain," Eleriss added. "But you will learn much."

"Goodie."

"We can start the lecture immediately," Jakatra said, "with physical activities beginning this evening."

While he spoke, Temi kept flexing her knee, putting weight on it from different angles. Despite her sarcasm and her determination not to get her hopes up too soon, she had to hide a grin that threatened as she jogged experimentally around the blanket. If her knee returned to 100 percent, she could play tennis again. She could train, compete, and *win* doing the one thing that she had always loved.

Her circuit brought her around to Eleriss and the stern-faced Jakatra.

"We will show you to your temporary home and the practice arena," Eleriss said.

Practice arena, not practice court. They had training in mind, too, just not the training she wanted to do. They had healed her so she could learn to poke holes into monsters. And she had agreed to that. She couldn't go back on her word, even if they would let her.

"Bring the sword," Jakatra said.

Temi smiled bleakly. She would go with them, but she would bide her time and hope... for a loophole.

3

"This will be your home while you train." Eleriss pointed at a door in the side of a big tree beside a meadow. Temi would have to duck to enter it, and unless that tree had a basement or a lot of levels, she couldn't imagine having room to do anything more than sleep inside. Even then, she wasn't sure she would be able to stretch her legs straight in the bed. If these people *had* beds. "There is food and water inside that should be acceptable to a human palate and digestive system," he added.

"Should?" Temi murmured.

"Our systems are similar. I sampled numerous cuisines in your world without suffering digestive stress."

"The flat disk covered with strange meat-like products was an exception," Jakatra muttered.

"Yes, pizza." Eleriss smiled brightly. "Pizza was digestively stressful."

"I don't doubt it." Temi pushed open the door to her tree house—what had Delia been saying about tree houses? It was as small inside as it had looked. The bed issue wouldn't be a problem, because something akin to a hammock appeared to be where one slept. The cushions on the floor in the back must be what passed for chairs, and the narrow counter with a jug of water, plate, bowl, and spoon must represent the kitchen. "Is this a normal... house for your people?"

"It is small and sparse," Eleriss said. "A place one would stay for training or for meditation. There is a pleasant stream down that path if you wish to do the latter, and Jakatra will meet you in the meadow every morning for training."

Jakatra had already started lecturing her about the hard work he would require as they walked through the forest to reach the meadow. Since the healer had left, they hadn't encountered another soul, though she had glimpsed animals grazing in a clearing, animals that reminded her of the black antelope she had seen in Africa.

"You will stay here when he's not training you," Eleriss said. "There are devices to keep dangerous animals away for a mile in each direction, but you must not go beyond their border."

"Because I'll be eaten, or because someone might see me and I'm not supposed to be here?"

Eleriss nodded. "Yes to both. In time, you should be able to protect yourself from the wildlife, but we have predatory species that are more aggressive than what your world possesses. That is the main reason you will be trained here. They will be good practice for the *jibtab*."

"The day grows long," Jakatra said. "We should begin."

Eleriss stepped back, extending his hand toward the meadow. "You are in charge here."

"You say I am in charge, but that I only have one week. You say I am in charge and that we will find a warrior with combat experience, but you choose a woman who has never held a weapon. You say I am in charge, but I am given no say in any of these decisions." Jakatra stalked to the meadow, his back rigid, his long ponytail twitching with his movements, like that of an agitated animal.

It was the most Temi had heard Jakatra say. By this point, she wasn't surprised by his agitation, but for the first time, she wondered if he might actually become an ally to her in this. If, after they trained for a while, he deemed her unfit, perhaps she would be sent back without the sword. Maybe she could even pretend to be more unfit than she was. The elves could then find someone else to protect the world, someone more experienced and appropriate. Delia would be disappointed—she and Simon actually seemed to *want* to battle monsters. But they wouldn't be able to if they didn't have the sword. Guns and bows had proved ineffective at harming the last one. Temi might even be saving their lives if her failure here forced the elves to find someone else to wield the weapon. Delia and Simon wouldn't be so foolish as to continue hunting creatures if they had no means of destroying them.

She'd no more than had the thought when she heard Simon's voice in her head, saying, "You're kidding, right?"

Funny, Temi hadn't known him that long, but she was sure those would be his exact words. Delia was more rational, but would she give up the hunt? Even if she did, she and Simon would still be out there in the sparsely populated mountains, searching for new archaeological sites and hunting for long-forgotten antiques they could sell in their business. If a monster found them, they would have no protection against it.

"She doesn't even listen, Eleriss," Jakatra growled.

Temi jumped. She had been staring off into the woods, unaware of her surroundings.

"I did mention to her that one could meditate here," Eleriss said.

Jakatra made a disgusted noise—or maybe it was a sign of that digestive stress they had been talking about. He was standing in the meadow, holding a sword. He hadn't had it before, and Temi hadn't noticed where it had come from.

"The sword, female." Jakatra pointed at her tennis bag.

"Bring it. Let's see if it hasn't decided to reject you as its owner after all." He looked wistful.

Despite her thoughts of using him as an ally, of deliberately failing whatever tests he had planned, his dismissal annoyed Temi. It made her want to prove him wrong about her capabilities.

Eleriss said something in a sharper tone that usual for him.

Maybe it was something about being more polite or not addressing her as "female," because Jakatra sighed and said, "Artemis, yes, fine. Artemis, bring the sword."

Normally, Temi would tell someone to use the short version of her name, since her grandmother and the reporters were the only ones who called her Artemis, but she didn't want to invite familiarity with Jakatra. She couldn't believe she had considered him attractive when she'd first seen them. That had been before he had spoken.

She unzipped her bag, pushed aside clothes and towels, and pulled the sword out of its scabbard. She should have taken the scabbard out first, because the serrated teeth on the back of the sharp, curving side of the blade snagged on something. Red panties. Temi stuffed them back in the bag, hoping the elves hadn't seen. Whatever race—or species—they were, they were still male, and some things didn't need to be shared with random males. Neither said a word, though. They were watching the sword, not the rest of her belongings.

As soon as her hand wrapped around the hilt, the blade lit up the afternoon shadows with its silver glow. That didn't surprise her, as it happened every time she picked it up. She hadn't figured out how to turn it off yet, short of putting it down.

Eleriss nodded to himself. Jakatra made a noise much like a sigh.

Chin up, Temi strode to the meadow. She was feigning confidence she didn't have, especially given that Jakatra's blade was as sharp and wicked as hers, even if it didn't glow. Shouldn't they start with wooden sticks or something? How far away did that healer live, in case she was in need of his services again?

"Any instructions?" Jakatra asked Eleriss. "Even though I'm in charge—" his lip twitched, "—I can't imagine you'll leave us here without further input."

"You are the master in this arena. Teach as you would teach anyone. Though the emphasis should be on animals more so than people. She'll need to defend herself against claws and teeth rather than swords. In addition to learning attack techniques, she will need to know how to determine where vital areas might be on a *jibtab*."

Jakatra looked at Temi. "Input," he mouthed, surprising her because, for a moment, it was as if they were on the same side and Eleriss was the outsider. No, she decided, Jakatra was just being sarcastic all around.

"Do as you will," Eleriss said, then frowned down at his pocket. He pulled something out, cupping it in his palm. So Temi wouldn't see it? He turned his back and walked away, speaking into the device.

"Artemis, do as I do." Jakatra bent his knees and tilted his torso away from her, leaving his sword arm toward her. "Ready stance."

Temi emulated him.

"We'll begin with basic footwork and the eight parries in the style I'm going to teach you."

Jakatra demonstrated footwork and defensive blocks with the sword for the next fifteen minutes, and Temi copied his moves. None of them were hard or complicated, and the ease with which her knee was supporting her made her want to bounce about and ask for more challenges, but she suspected the difficulty level would increase once he started whacking at her with his sword. Eleriss returned before they reached that stage. Even if their expressions weren't quite human, Temi thought she read grimness on his face. At the least, his usual cheer was absent.

"Problem?" Jakatra asked.

"A message from my father," Eleriss said.

"Oh? Has he learned of your project?" Jakatra tilted his sword toward Temi.

"I don't know, but I must speak with him. Continue with her, please. I will come check on your progress tomorrow."

Temi watched him leave with a touch of trepidation. She wasn't sure how far she trusted either of the elves, but Eleriss was definitely the more pleasant of the two. Spending time alone with Jakatra in the middle of a forest as it was getting dark wouldn't have been her first choice on how to spend the evening.

As the training continued, however, he remained professional. Aloof, but professional.

After teaching her how to use her thoughts to turn off the sword's glow—apparently it would cut through his regular sword if she didn't do so—he drilled her over and over on the eight parries and what he called advances, lunges, and retreats. With most of the footwork, there was something similar in tennis, and she had no trouble covering the ground quickly, though he corrected her technique often. The parries weren't similar to racket work, so she had to concentrate on them, especially when it came to figuring out which block to use against which attack. At the speed he was going—obviously a training pace rather than his normal capability—she could get the sword across in time to bat away his attack, one way or another, but with far too much flustered flailing. He would explain what the correct parry should have been, then repeat the exact same attack at least fifty times. Temi accepted the repetition without comment; every sport had it.

By the time full darkness fell, sweat drenched her body, and her limbs had the strength of noodles. Her knee ached, and she wasn't sure if it was a sign that her recovery hadn't been as complete as she'd hoped or if the muscles that she had been favoring for so long were simply exhausted from this exercise. Temi hadn't seen anything that looked like a shower in her tree house; she hoped she had simply missed it on her first perusal and that it was tucked into a corner. Along with a sauna and a masseuse.

Jakatra backed away and lowered his sword. "Enough. You will rest now."

Good. It was probably close to dawn by now back in Arizona. Her attempt to nod at Jakatra turned into a yawn.

Floating lights had gone on at some point, hovering in the air around the meadow. Temi decided not to find it creepy that she hadn't noticed them during the day and that they weren't supported by posts or wires, at least not as far as she could tell.

"I will return in the morning. Dawn." Without waiting for an answer, he strode across the meadow and into the woods, disappearing into the undergrowth.

Temi could only stare after him, having no idea how she had fared for a first timer. Was she pathetic compared to his lithe people? A disappointment? Or had she done enough right to make him feel he wasn't wasting his time? From his corrections, one would never know. The closest he'd come to praise was to say, "Yes," about once an hour when she managed to get the right block to work at the same time as the right footwork. Something more... encouraging might have been nice. Despite her earlier thoughts about throwing the game—pretending to be worse than she was—she hadn't been able to go through with it. She hadn't wanted the damned elf to think any less of her than he already did. It shouldn't matter, but for some reason it did.

She wished Delia had been allowed to come. Her commentary would have been more entertaining at least, and she probably would have enjoyed learning about swordsmanship too. Temi hadn't hated it—the sport element and the challenge of improving appealed to her—but she had a hard time forgetting that the end goal was to learn not just how to defend herself but to kill things with the blade.

The floating lights dimmed, and she took that as a sign that she needed to get some food and some sleep. A screech sounded in the distance, the cry of something large. Something predatory. Another reason to go inside and lock the door. If it had a lock.

4

Temi woke from a heavy sleep, lurching into a sitting position and almost falling out of the hammock as she clutched her chest. Her heart hammered at her ribs, and her disorientated brain couldn't remember where she was or why. A chilling cry pierced the walls of her room, something between a screech and a roar. The noise filled her with terror, and she stared at the darkness around her, primitive instincts telling her to hide, but where?

A silvery glow arose on the other side of the tiny room. After a moment of confusion, she remembered what it was, remembered everything. By the time a second cry reverberated through the night, she had climbed out of the hammock and clasped her hand around the sword hilt.

"One mile," she breathed, "wasn't that what he said? That dangerous animals wouldn't come closer than a mile?"

Whatever was making those cries—from the different pitches, she thought more than one creature might be involved—they sounded closer than a mile. She would like to think Eleriss and Jakatra wouldn't bring her all the way here, bribe a doctor, and spend time training her, only to let her be devoured by the local equivalent of ravenous wolves. And yet...

Another high-pitched roar emanated from the forest.

"Definitely not a mile away." Temi rested her hand on the back of the door, somewhat reassured by the solidness of the wood. There was no lock, she had found, but the latch was sturdy. The wise thing to do would be to wait inside the tree, in case that protective border the elves had mentioned wasn't quite as protective as they thought.

A scream penetrated her tree home, and she jerked her head up. That was different from the other cries. It had sounded human. Or maybe elven. Was someone out there? Being hunted? Eleriss? What if he had come back to check on her and had run into trouble? She had been worried that Jakatra thought little of her ability to learn swordsmanship. What would he think if he found his comrade dead and horribly mauled on her doorstep? He would know she had done nothing to stop it.

Temi chewed on her lip, wishing the elves had told her more about this world, about these predators.

The scream came again. Male or female, she couldn't tell, but it definitely sounded like a person. And that person was terrified.

Temi looked down at the glowing sword. "If you can kill monsters on Earth, I hope that means you can kill rabid wolves here." She further hoped the wolves, or whatever was out there, would oblige by attacking in a manner that matched up with the blocks she had been taught, because she wasn't ready for extemporizing.

Taking a deep breath, Temi unlatched the door. The lights in the meadow had turned off, and darkness smothered the forest. The cries of the predators came again, from somewhere on the other side of her meadow. Maybe it was her imagination, but those cries seemed more eager than before, closer to the kill.

Temi stalked into the meadow, clutching the sword in front of her like a shield, trying to spot movement in the undergrowth. She had no idea how to track anything in the woods, especially at night. She needed a sign to guide her.

The sign came sooner than she expected. Two hulking black figures ran out of the shadows on two legs. They were bear-sized and shaggy, with clawed digits that reminded her more of hands than paws. Animal-like snouts lifted, sniffing the air, and then the creatures charged in her direction. Their gleaming yellow eyes burned into her soul.

There was no sign of the person Temi had come out to help. The screams had stopped. Was she too late?

As the shaggy animals raced across the meadow at her, she thought of sprinting back to the tree house and slamming the door, hoping it was enough to protect her, but they were less than twenty meters away and closing the distance quickly. She couldn't outrun them, couldn't make it back in time. She would have to stand her ground.

She lifted the sword, bringing it back over her shoulder so she could whip it toward them, rotating her body into the attack. She had no idea if that was the right technique, but Jakatra hadn't gotten around to attacks yet.

"Bastard," she muttered, sinking down, feeling the support of the earth beneath her feet, readying herself to meet the assault.

Temi was a heartbeat from swinging when the two creatures split and veered in opposite directions, breaking around her like a river around a boulder. Afraid they intended to surround her, she ran forward and whirled, so she could keep both of them within sight. But they didn't turn back toward her. They sped across the meadow and ran into the forest. She thought she caught the gleam of something tiny glowing high up on one's back, but the trees soon hid the creatures from sight.

She turned again, remembering the distressed cry and intending to try to find the person. But a lean dark figure was walking toward her, this one far less shaggy than the animals. A hand waved, and the lights around the meadow turned on. Jakatra.

Temi glanced in the direction the animal with the glowing something-or-other had gone. Its placement reminded her of the microchips dogs received. Could that have been some kind of chip? Embedded to control the creatures?

She lowered the sword when Jakatra stopped in front of her.

"A test?" she asked.

"A test," he agreed.

She didn't know whether to feel annoyed or flabbergasted, or both, but she waited in silence for his assessment. Had she passed? Or had she been too slow? Had she waited too long to come outside and help that person—a person who presumably didn't exist or who had been part of the hoax? Or maybe she should have taken the attack to the creatures, rushing and striking at them instead of waiting for them to come to her.

"It is over," Jakatra said brusquely. He sounded more annoyed than usual. "Return to sleep."

Temi gaped at him. Oh, sure. Like it would be so easy to go back to sleep now. And what the hell? He wasn't even going to tell her if she had passed? Or what exactly the scenario had been designed to test?

"Wait," she blurted when he turned away.

Jakatra didn't say a word, but he faced her again.

"What was I supposed to do? Did I pass?" She hated that she sounded like a school kid, asking if she had done well enough to go out to recess, but after being jerked out of her bed in the middle of the night and terrified half to death, didn't she have a right to know?

A long moment passed as Jakatra stared at her. Just when she was certain he wouldn't answer, he said, "You passed."

What? If she had passed, why was he so irritated?

Temi had no sooner had the thought than the answer came to her. Oh. "You didn't want me to, did you?"

"No."

Well. He was a bastard, but he was an honest bastard.

"You wanted the Greek guy," Temi said, thinking of the ancient warrior who had been uncovered and revived in that cave, only to escape before the elves could talk him into helping.

"I wanted no one," Jakatra said coolly. "*This—*" he gestured at her, or maybe the sword, "—is a pointless use of my time and talents. I care nothing for a people that are intelligent enough to realize their species has overshot the carrying capacity of their world but too selfish and lazy to do anything about it. Your entire race is going to be extinct within a century, and you're taking the rest of the species on your planet with you. Helping you stop a few predators right now... it's meaningless. What will it matter in the end? What Eleriss thinks this can possibly accomplish, I cannot begin to guess."

"Hey, don't hold back for my sake," Temi said, stunned by his vitriol. "Say what you really feel."

He frowned, probably not understanding the sarcasm, but had a response anyway. "That is how *most* of the galaxy feels. Do you know why you're not welcome here? Everyone is terrified that your people will figure out a way off your rock and do it all again." He flexed a hand toward the stars. "Eleriss and those like him are optimistic fools."

"Then why are you taking orders from him?"

Jakatra's eyes chilled a few degrees. "They are not orders. My family has worked with his for many generations. *Most* of them are great scholars, worthy colleagues. But Eleriss is young. Foolish."

Temi didn't know what to say about the insult, about *any* of his insults. Delia or Simon would have a smart response. She sighed with disappointment at herself.

"Return to your rest," Jakatra said and started to leave once again.

"No," Temi blurted before she could think better of it.

"What?"

"I've slept long enough. If you're out here thinking up tests for me, you've obviously slept long enough too." She waved the sword. His dismissal of her pissed her off; his dismissal of all of humanity pissed her off too. She wanted to show him he was wrong. The only way she could. "Let's get back to training."

Temi expected him to scoff and walk away. His long assessing stare made her uncomfortable, but she forced herself to meet that cool gaze.

"You promised Eleriss to work with me for a week, right? I want my entire week."

"If that is your wish," he said softly.

Something about his tone, or maybe the dark glint in his eyes, made her think he planned to make her regret her decision. So be it. It wouldn't be the first thing in life she regretted.

5

Temi was sure there had been another time in her life when she had been this tired, but she couldn't remember it. Though she wanted to, she couldn't muster the strength to try another series of attacks on Jakatra. That morning, he had shown her how to use the curved blade of her sword, as well as the serrated teeth on the back side, and he had insisted she repeat the moves over and over again, as she had done with the parries. They had begun sparring then, exchanging blows like real fighters, but it was hours later now, and she could barely lift her blade to ward off his attacks. Even that was becoming harder, with her legs quivering like Jell-O.

Her stomach was growling, and she desperately needed a break, but how could she ask for one after demanding Jakatra stay up half the night training her? If he was tired, it didn't show up in *his* moves. And *he* had no trouble mounting attacks.

After knocking her onto her ass for the five hundredth time that day, Jakatra backed away and raised a hand, his signal to stop. Maybe he had been reading her thoughts. Or maybe he could simply tell she was about to fall over. Or throw up. Or fall over while throwing up.

"You are making progress," came a voice from the side of the meadow.

Destiny Unchosen

Temi was too tired to twitch in surprise. Eleriss stood there, wearing loose beiges and browns instead of the black leather jacket and dark clothing she had always seen him in.

"Get water," Jakatra told Temi and walked toward Eleriss.

She held back a grimace. She wanted him to order her to fall into her hammock and sleep for twenty hours, not simply to have a five-minute water break. Nonetheless, she staggered to the side of the meadow and flopped next to her water jug. She thought about heading into the tree house to find some of the semi-palatable, greenish-gray wafers she had eaten for breakfast, but she hadn't seen Eleriss since the day before, since some call from his family had taken him away, and she wanted to know what had happened. And if it had to do with her.

"She passed your test last night?" Eleriss asked, looking at her and being polite enough to speak in English.

"Yes," Jakatra said. He still didn't sound happy about it, but at this point, Temi expected all of his responses to sound grumpy. If there was something in the world, this one or another one, that pleased him, she couldn't guess what it might be.

"Excellent." Eleriss smiled, as unfazed as always with Jakatra's surliness. "She is clearly tired, but she appears farther along than I dared hope. On that last riposte, she almost hit you."

Had she? Everything was a blur. Temi hardly remembered any of the individual encounters.

"She did not," Jakatra said stiffly.

Eleriss's smile grew wider. "I have eyes, my friend."

"Many inches parted us. I was in no danger of being struck." Jakatra switched to his own language then, asking a question, it sounded like, and Eleriss responded in his own tongue as well.

Temi pushed herself to her feet and did her best not to

wobble as she headed to the tree to retrieve one of those wafers. They had a vegetable-like taste but had protein and fat in them, as well, she believed, since they stuck with her longer than she would have expected, especially given all the work she was doing. This world's equivalent of an energy bar. Inside, she sank down on a cushion for a moment, wiping her sweat with a towel, and relaxing, out of sight of the elves, for a moment. The night before, she had discovered a washing device in the kitchen that reminded her of the hand showers in Europe. At least it had given her a chance to bathe, though the effects had long since worn off.

The food gave her some fresh energy, and she wandered back outside to find the elves still talking. They stopped when she approached, and Eleriss looked at her.

"Jakatra says you are progressing marvelously."

"Somehow I doubt that was the word he used," Temi said. "Even allowing for a very loose translation."

"I told him your footwork is passable," Jakatra told her. Yes, that sounded more like him. Actually, it was the biggest sign of approval she'd received from him. Maybe he felt coerced to make the statement because of Eleriss's presence.

"You said it was *surprisingly* passable given how few hours she's trained," Eleriss said.

Jakatra stretched his fingers in some gesture of dismissal. Or maybe it was an announcement that he was done with the argument.

Eleriss nodded to Temi. "I thought it might be the case when I read about your sport. With the stick and the ball. Sports can be a good way to learn coordination and balance."

Temi tried not to feel like he was talking down to her. She didn't want to offend her only cheerleader here. "Yes, I've heard that."

"It is likely that you'll be able to continue your training for a few days more," Eleriss said.

"Nobody's found out I'm here yet?"

"Correct. My own long absences from the family have been questioned, but that is for me to worry about."

"Nobody's missed Jakatra?" Temi asked. He had been gone as long as Eleriss, and he was spending all of this time with her. What if someone came looking for *him*? And what happened if someone who wasn't a part of this little help-the-humans program found her anyway? Jakatra's rant from the night before made her wonder if she might be in danger of more than deportation.

"My presence is not requested at political or social gatherings." Jakatra flicked a hand toward Eleriss. Implying his was?

"Oh? Are you grumpy around your own people too?"

Jakatra gave her a grumpy look for a response.

"Artemis, let us talk a moment." Eleriss headed toward the trees and waved for her to follow.

Jakatra frowned but turned his back and propped his hands on his hips. For some reason, Temi hesitated, reluctant to go off and have a private conversation without him. It wasn't as if these last twenty-four hours had caused them to form some lasting coach-student bond—that hadn't gone well for her last coach, and she'd be loath to inflict it on anyone else, species regardless—but at the same time, she found herself reluctant to speak about him behind his back. Maybe Eleriss wouldn't have that in mind.

"I know Jakatra can be… grumpy," Eleriss said as soon as she joined him. So much for her hope. "But are you being treated fairly? Is your house adequate?"

She gazed over at Jakatra, whose back was still to them, thinking of all the times she had mentally screamed at him in her mind during their marathon training session.

She might not like him much, but she wouldn't call him unfair. "Everything is fine."

"Please learn what you can from him, but do not allow him to deflate your spirit. He was born a pessimist."

"Yes, I've gotten that impression." And that he hated humans. "May I ask you a question?" Temi asked, not wanting to discuss Jakatra further. She wasn't even sure they had moved far enough away to keep him from hearing. Who knew what the points on those ears did? He might have twice the auditory range of a human for all she knew.

Eleriss did his signature head tilt. "Yes."

"Can you tell from here if my friends are all right? Or if there's another monster out there to worry about? You've implied several times that more would be coming."

"And you're eager to return and combat them?" Eleriss asked brightly.

Uh, right. She decided not to mention her thoughts of intentionally flunking the training so she could go back to the tennis circuit. "I apparently have the only sword that can fight them here. I'm afraid they might try to do something about a monster if one showed up, even if they weren't properly equipped."

"Yes, they are curious humans."

Temi wasn't sure whether he meant curious as in nosey or curious as in strange and unique specimens. Either could apply.

"A new *jibtab* has not yet appeared," Eleriss said.

"Good."

"It may happen soon though. I fear many will be coming."

"You said you don't know who's responsible for them?" Temi got the feeling he knew a lot more than he had told her or Delia. Might it even be one of his people? Or... She frowned at Jakatra, remembering his implication that there were numerous races in the galaxy, none impressed with humanity.

"I do not," Eleriss said. "If I did, perhaps I could... " He paused and contemplated the grass at his feet. "No, perhaps not. I cannot act openly unless... Politics, you understand. We cannot interfere. It is true we used to visit your world, but it has since been agreed—a very strict law was made..." He grimaced. Remembering that he was violating this law? "We cannot have anything to do with your people. Not anymore. But I thought if we could point you to a useful weapon that already existed on your planet, from a visitor of old, then it would not violate certain rules about interference."

Temi thought about pointing out that bringing someone here to train with that weapon might be construed as interference. But Eleriss doubtlessly already knew he was walking a fine line with his people.

"It is unfortunate we cannot give you far more training," Eleriss said, "but a week is as long as I dare keep you here. Also, you are right to be concerned for your people. More danger is coming."

"Is there a reason we have to stay here to train?" Temi waved toward Jakatra. "We have meadows on Earth too. Granted, Arizona's meadows are on the dusty side, but that shouldn't matter." She would rather not stay here if there was a chance someone would stumble across her presence and find it less than pleasing.

"Your world lacks suitable predators to train on. You will move from combating Jakatra to combating dangerous animals soon."

"Like the black shaggy things from last night?"

"Yes, except bigger and fiercer. Those were domesticated."

How comforting. Even though she didn't say it out loud, he must have guessed her concern.

"Do not worry. Jakatra will train you first and watch from nearby when you confront these animals. You will do well. I am certain."

Temi would be more comforted if Jakatra was the one saying that.

"I wonder if it was indeed an accident that brought you to us," Eleriss mused. "Humans also believe in... what is the word in your tongue? Fate?"

Temi nodded, though she had no idea what the original term was he was trying to define.

"I believe you'll be a good champion for your world."

A champion for her world? What a thought.

"You barely know me." Or so she assumed. If he had researched her—and he had mentioned tennis—then he might know far more than she would have liked.

"You are calm," Eleriss said. "In many situations. When Jakatra is pressing you aggressively. Also, the night you slew the *jibtab*. You seemed almost indifferent to that accomplishment."

How could he know that? He and Jakatra hadn't been there to witness that underwater fight.

"I'm not serene. I'm just..." Not that invested in this, Temi thought. Was that it? Not exactly, but the last time she had wept for joy had been when she won Wimbledon, and the last time she had wept for sorrow had been the same night, after her coach's death. Everything since then had affected her less profoundly. Or maybe all the reporters, all the questions, and all the anger directed at her had forced her to wall herself off, to stop feeling. "I've been through a lot in the last couple of years. I think I'm just numb to everything anymore."

Eleriss did not respond, but he gazed thoughtfully after her when she headed back to the meadow. Jakatra had his sword out and appeared ready for more training. Temi braced herself. She had better be too.

6

Temi had never been on a hovercraft, but the vehicle Eleriss drove through the trees fit the name. The truck-sized craft had a pair of seats up front, where the elves sat, and a cargo area in the back with two benches along the sides. Temi sat on one, watching the forest as the craft, floating several feet off the ground, zipped in and out of the trees.

Birds squawked at their passing. There was more wildlife out here than there had been near Temi's meadow, including bird-sized insects. Something that looked like a flying tarantula landed on Jakatra's shoulder. He brushed it off, as if it were of less consequence than a mosquito. Temi gulped. If the insects were that big, what kinds of higher-order predators would be lurking out here?

Here and there, narrow animal trails meandered through the brush, but Temi had yet to see anything that qualified as a road. She had yet to see a house, either, aside from her small tree abode. The elves had to be deliberately keeping her out in the wilderness so no one would see her. Delia would be peppering them with questions about their world, how populous it was, how many languages they spoke, and Temi felt remiss for not asking such things. Jakatra probably wouldn't answer, but Eleriss might. But she had other things on her mind.

It was nearing the end of her fifth day here, and for the first time, Jakatra had let her sleep in. Because they were to hunt tonight. Temi would have been more enthused at the prospect of hunting during daylight hours, but the pale yellow sun was setting, the trees casting shadows miles long on the forest floor.

To the side of the hovercraft, leaves rustled, and wood cracked. Something large bounded through the brush. Neither of the elves did more than glance in that direction, but whatever was making the noise didn't go away. It paralleled them, crashing through the foliage and keeping up with easy lopes. The leaves obscured it, but Temi glimpsed long, powerful legs, a broad head and snout, and sleek fur. It was bigger than the domesticated bear things that had been part of her first test.

The sword rested between Temi's knees, and she wrapped her hand around the hilt. She leaned toward the elves. "Is that what we're hunting?" Another branch snapped. Or maybe that was a *trunk* being knocked over. "And, ah, is the hunt going to start soon?"

"Not until tonight," Eleriss said over his shoulder. "This *aramushua*—truck?—is protected. It is unlikely the *uruvneshi* will attack." Apparently that second word didn't have a translation. No Earth equivalent.

"But we won't be protected when we hunt?" Temi asked.

"No." Jakatra climbed into the rear of the hovercraft and sat across from her, putting his back to the creature. "We evolved here, alongside these predators. They used to hunt us until we developed weapons and armor to thwart their attacks. They can tell when we carry these protections with us, and they do not attack, because they would be harmed. Mildly harmed, but it is enough to convince them to leave us be. Our swords will not have this effect on them, even yours."

"Because they know they can beat us if all we have are swords?"

"They will believe so, yes."

"Because they've beaten a lot of sword fighters in past ages?" Temi wondered if many of Jakatra's people still wandered around with swords. He obviously knew what he was doing, but was it actually common? It would seem strange from a people who could travel between worlds and heal wounds that could stump the best surgeons.

"They have," Jakatra said.

"A lot of women, children, and men, also," Eleriss said. "They find the taste of our flesh particularly appealing. Our ancestors had to be crafty survivalists to evolve on this world. One wonders if today's generation would be so able."

Jakatra looked at the back of Eleriss's head with hooded eyes, as if to say he was *plenty* crafty, thank you. Temi hoped that would be the case, since they were to be dropped off in this forest to hunt—or be hunted—without any of the superior protections Eleriss had mentioned.

"If they're that dangerous—" judging by the size of the one loping along beside them, Temi couldn't imagine them being anything but dangerous, "—and you now have the technology to deal with them, why not eradicate them?"

Jakatra's face grew flinty as his eyes turned back toward her. Even mild-mannered Eleriss frowned back at Temi, and she shifted on the hard bench, knowing she had said the wrong thing.

"To eradicate a species would be a heinous crime," Eleriss said.

"But hunting a species for the purpose of training, that's fine?" Temi asked, feeling a touch defensive at their angry—no, disappointed—expressions.

Eleriss held up a device, the one Temi had guessed was the equivalent of a phone a few days earlier. "We have surveyed the numbers and placement of all species of wildlife in the area and have chosen a hunting ground based on this information. To kill a couple of the large predators in the area will not detrimentally impact the ecosystem."

Temi wondered if they had gotten permission to hunt the creatures or if she was going on the equivalent of a poaching trip in some big elven park.

The hovercraft slowed down. If they had arrived at a destination with something significant about it, it wasn't apparent to her. More trees, more bushes, and more rustling undergrowth surrounded them. A bevy of large birds flapped out of a large shrub as they drew to a stop nearby. At least whatever had been chasing the craft had disappeared, or it had stopped tearing through the brush after them, anyway.

Jakatra grabbed his sword and a bag and hopped to the ground, landing lightly in a patch of low ferns. "Come," he told Temi.

Eleriss hopped out of the vehicle, too, though he left it running, its engine making a soft *putch-putch* noise as it idled. Temi had no idea what powered it. She didn't smell any exhaust.

Aware of Jakatra watching her, she climbed over the side of the craft, her sword in hand. It glowed more than usual, brightening the shadows deepening amongst the trees. Maybe it knew danger lurked nearby.

"You do not wish me to retrieve you until the morning, correct?" Eleriss asked.

"Yes," Jakatra said.

Did Eleriss's expression grow a touch doubtful? "You are certain you don't wish me to stay nearby?"

"Yes."

"It is possible you will be overwhelmed. The *sarushnaka* can smell our blood from miles away."

"I am aware of this. They are territorial, so it is unlikely we would face more than a female and its mate, at the most." Jakatra pointed to the hovercraft. "The sooner you leave, the sooner we can begin training."

Eleriss hesitated, then tilted his head. His "yes" tilt was a little different from his "I'm confused" tilt. "As you wish." He looked at them both and said, "What is the phrase? Have luck?"

"Good luck," Temi said.

"Yes. Good luck. And do not play with each other's bodies."

Temi almost dropped her sword. "What?"

It wasn't as if she had never heard sexual innuendo before; it was just that she hadn't heard any of it from either of the elves, and she wondered if she had misunderstood. Or maybe Eleriss had translated something poorly. Jakatra didn't look confused by the statement though. He merely gave his buddy a flat look.

"There is a tale among our people," Eleriss said, "that speaks of young lovers going out into the wilderness to find privacy from disapproving family members, only to become distracted by their ardor and turn into easy prey for predators."

"We're not planning any ardor," Temi hurried to say.

Did Eleriss think there had been something more than sword training going on out in the woods? As if she would have any interest in someone who thought humans were idiots and had been so dismissive of the idea that one of his people had apparently found one of her ancestors appealing.

"No?" Eleriss asked. "Females usually find Jakatra attractive."

"I don't." Not exactly true, but... "Even if I did, I wouldn't do anything that could get him hurt out here. The last time something like that happened, I lost my coach." She shook her head, trying to push away the memories that rushed into her mind, memories she had already relived far too many times.

It was only then, in glancing at Jakatra's sour expression and Eleriss's surprised one, that Temi realized he had been teasing them. Or teasing Jakatra, more specifically. Her cheeks heated with embarrassment. Why had she answered them so seriously—so personally?

"No ardor," Jakatra confirmed. "Only hunting." He turned his back on them and strode away from the hovercraft.

"Be careful," Eleriss said, more somber now. "We do not have time to train another, and I have heard... it is possible your presence on our world has been noticed. We will need to send you home soon. Before you are in danger from more than hungry animals."

Just in case she hadn't had enough to worry about.

Temi followed Jakatra into the brush, her hand clenched tightly about her sword.

7

TEMI WAITED, KNEES BENT SLIGHTLY, weight resting on the balls of her feet. Just like getting ready to return a serve. Except the thing racing toward her at a hundred miles an hour wasn't a tennis ball; it was a shaggy brown animal with fangs like daggers.

It pounded through the shadows on four legs, crushing foliage with heavy paws, ignoring branches that scraped at its fur, staring at her with hungry yellow eyes. Every instinct told Temi to run, but Jakatra had warned her not to turn her back, that it would sense her fear and pounce. As if it wasn't going to pounce now. It was covering the ground as fast as a car on the highway, its maw opening wide in anticipation.

Twenty meters. Ten meters.

Sweat dampened her palms. An image of the weapon being torn from her grip popped into her mind, but there was no time to wipe her hands. She squeezed down on the hilt.

Five meters. Temi held her stance, waiting until it was too late for the creature to alter its course.

It leapt into the air, paws stretching toward her. A throaty snarl burst from its throat. Claws like switchblades sprang from its digits.

"Now," Jakatra ordered from a nearby tree.

Temi was already springing to the side, whipping the sword at the creature's shoulder as she did so. The throat would have been an ideal target, but its limbs were longer than hers, and she couldn't hit it as she sprang away. But a wound was a start. Setting up the point so she could take advantage.

Her blade sliced into the flesh of its shoulder, as she had hoped, but the blow didn't keep it from twisting in the air and swinging at her with one of those massive paws. Temi jumped back again, jerking her head to avoid those slashing claws. She landed on sure feet, glad she had studied the ground and knew there was nothing behind her that would entangle her. She backed up further, to a tree the thickness of an aged redwood.

The creature spun toward her. Dark purple blood spattered the rich green leaves of the dense undergrowth, but the beast showed no sign of pain. It bunched its muscles, preparing to spring again. Temi thought about sidestepping away from the tree, so she could leap away in any direction, but it could be a useful shield too. Or... she glanced up, spotting a branch eight or nine feet high. Maybe she could—

The creature attacked again before she had time to finalize her battle plan. This time, it roared and charged her without jumping, barreling straight at her like a train. She almost let its speed and ferocity set her back on her heels, but she would be defending from a position of desperation if she allowed that. Instead, she kept her weight even until it was almost upon her, then she jumped into the air, catching the branch with her free hand and curling her legs up at the same time as she slammed down with the sword, aiming for its skull this time.

The creature's shoulder bumped her foot as it passed, jostling her aim. Her weapon slashed through its ear and sheared fur and flesh off its head, but it wasn't the killing blow she had hoped for.

Disgusted, Temi decided she needed to attack from a solid spot on the ground instead of flailing at it while airborne. Then she could push off the earth and throw her hips, her entire body, behind her swings. The snarling beast spun about, not yet slowed by its injuries. It didn't even seem to notice them.

She dropped from the branch to face it. Instead of charging at her again, it circled her and the tree, keeping its body low as it sought the right moment.

"Go ahead," Temi whispered. "I'm staying put this time."

The animal lunged toward her, and she shifted her weight, ready to throw everything into a swing at it, but the lunge was only a feint. Her furry opponent was testing her. She took a couple of steps toward it, waving the sword, thinking *she* might get a chance to charge. Or at least hoping the weapon's silvery glow might unsettle the animal. Faster than she ever could be, the creature didn't let her get close. Not on her terms anyway.

Temi stepped on a branch and the wood snapped. A small animal sprang out of a nearby bush, startling her. For an instant, her attention was drawn away from the creature. It chose that moment to charge again, leaping toward her head—toward her *neck*.

Temi wanted to spring away from those raking claws, but she made herself sink low and stand her ground. She ducked under the outstretched paws, then came up from beneath them, pushing off the ground and throwing her blade at the creature's neck. The sword sliced through flesh, muscle, and bone, like a knife cutting warm butter, but she was buried beneath hundreds of pounds of animal before she could tell if she'd struck a killing blow.

No claws or fangs cut into her, but fear boiled into her throat as she was borne to the ground. The creature thrashed, and she didn't know if it was dying or attacking her. She squirmed, trying to scramble out, to escape, but the damned thing had to weigh a half ton. Her knee screamed as she twisted it, and it wasn't even the one that usually bothered her. Gasping, she finally clawed her way to freedom. She crawled, trying to put distance between herself and the animal and finally found her feet. Somehow, she had maintained a grip on the sword. Her hands were covered in blood, and she gulped, but the animal wasn't moving. It was a good thing. If it had been alive, it could have smothered her to death by simply not letting her escape. Forget the claws and teeth.

"Next time, get in, make the killing blow, and then get out before it falls on you," came Jakatra's comment from a few feet away. He was leaning against the tree on the other side of the dead animal.

Temi bit back a comment that would have been along the lines of, screw you. She brushed dirt off her clothes, to give herself a moment to calm down—though the action was pointless when those clothes were already stained with blood—then managed a civil, "Yes, I figured out that my strategy was flawed as I was being smashed into the ground."

Jakatra gazed blandly at her. "What will you do differently next time?"

No congratulations on killing it, however messily. No *good job* for not losing her sword under a half-ton dead monster. No promise that she had passed her first test. Temi sighed.

"I'm not sure," she said. "I thought I had to get in close to really land a good whack, but that probably wasn't the smartest thing, after all. If I hadn't killed it, I would have been dead."

"Yes."

Such charming bluntness.

"I wasn't doing much damage by jumping in and out, trying to hurt it without getting inside its range," Temi said. "I was afraid if I kept messing around like that, I'd get unlucky and it would catch me. And the wounds I'd inflicted weren't doing much to slow it down. Losing its ear didn't faze it at all."

"Eventually, you would have worn it down with that strategy."

"So that's what I should have done?" Temi imagined tripping over a root during a prolonged battle.

"With practice, you will find a style that suits you for hunting big game. That is why we are here."

Standing behind a ridge and shooting big game with a grenade launcher sounded like a style that would suit her. The elves claimed that even powerful Earth-based weapons wouldn't work on the monsters, but she wasn't sure she believed that. Simon didn't. The last time she had seen him, he had been shopping online for materials to make explosives, proclaiming that all of the *components* were perfectly legal to own.

"The attrition style will likely be a necessity with the *jibtab*. Vital targets may not be obvious, and what appears to be a neck might not carry blood."

Yes, the creature they had faced before hadn't even seemed to *have* blood. Simon and Delia had speculated that it was more robot than being, though even that hadn't been a very accurate classification. "Burying it under a million tons of rock and water worked."

"In that instance, yes, but you will not always be able to choose the place where you face a *jibtab*. And it, too, may be different each time, made from different raw materials, depending on the whims of its creator."

The way he spoke authoritatively about creators and materials made Temi wonder if he and Eleriss had been telling the truth, that they didn't know who was making the monsters.

"With that sword, you'll cut through muscle and bone much more easily than you would with mine." Jakatra waved the blade he had brought with him, the same one he had been training with all week. "The attrition style should prove effective."

An eerie sound drifted through the forest, something between a groan and a howl. It made the hair on Temi's arms stand up.

"Next test?" she asked.

How many battles would Jakatra expect from her that night? With drying sweat and blood caking her, all she wanted was a shower and a bed. She already felt as if she had played an entire match, and full darkness had yet to fall, something that would add a degree of difficulty to her encounters, glowing sword or not.

"The *saru*," Jakatra said, his pointed ears tilted toward the noise. "Odd."

"How so?" Other than the fact that those howls made her want to crawl into a bank vault and lock herself in.

"They compete for territory with the *uruv-neshi*." He pointed at the dead animal. "They'll fight if they encounter one another, so it's unusual to find them within ten miles of each other."

Another howl stirred Temi's arm hairs. "Maybe this one knows this territory is newly available."

"Perhaps." Jakatra didn't sound convinced. She tried not to find that disturbing. "Regardless, a *saru* would be a good test. They are much faster than the *uruv-neshi*."

Temi still didn't know how she had fared on the *last* test. Was killing the beast and surviving enough for a satisfactory rating? Or would she lose points for being smashed under a corpse?

A second howl joined the first, this one an even higher and creepier pitch. Temi wanted to remain calm. She had fought one creature and won, so she could handle this new challenge—she knew she could—but she could feel her heart racing in her chest, hammering against her ribs. Aside from the howls, the forest was so still that she could hear her own breathing, short, quick inhalations. Damn, she wasn't calm at all.

"Two?" Jakatra frowned. "Even odder. They are not pack animals."

"Are they drawn to the smell of blood? Maybe we should move away from the corpse."

"They prefer that their food still be alive when they dine." Jakatra did walk away from the first dead animal, though, heading toward the open area where they had waited for their first attacker. "Come. I will assist you in this next battle."

Well, that was something anyway.

Temi jogged after him, sticking close. The howls were continuing. And they were growing closer. "Do you want to use this sword?" she asked, having the sense that his wasn't magical or specially powered or whatever it was that made hers glow.

He gazed back at her silvery blade. "No, it is yours to master."

More howls joined the first, and his head spun toward the noise. "More?" he whispered, a note of concern in his voice for the first time.

The cries were blending together now to Temi's ears, and she couldn't tell if there were two creatures or ten. "How many?"

Jakatra stopped walking. "There are at least four."

"Four animals as big and strong as what I just fought?"

"Not quite as big, but stronger and faster. And they never travel in packs. Or even pairs. The female kills the male after they mate if he doesn't leave her side soon enough."

"They sound cozy."

Jakatra didn't answer; he was looking in all directions, analyzing the forest, his eyes glowing faintly in the deepening gloom. Searching for somewhere to hide? To run to?

"Jakatra?" she whispered during a lull in the howls. The woods were utterly silent around them. "Did you bring any of your superior protections that drive them away? For backup?"

His expression changed little, but she got a sense of bleakness from them. "If I had, they wouldn't have come."

"Do you have a way to communicate with Eleriss?"

"No."

The howls grew shorter, more excited, reminding Temi of coyotes on the heels of their prey. Except these creatures sounded much bigger than coyotes.

"They're here." Jakatra pointed into the trees.

It was too dark now for Temi to pick out anything—the silvery illumination from her sword didn't reach that far—but she trusted he could see with his glowing eyes.

"Come, up that big tree. Can you climb it? There are too many for us to fight."

"I'll figure it out."

Temi raced after him to a tree with a six-foot-diameter trunk. It looked sturdy enough to withstand even the most determined predator. So long as none of them came armed with chainsaws.

The cracked plates of bark reminded Temi of alligator junipers back home, but the trunk rose straight up without any branches for the first twenty feet. Not fazed, Jakatra charged up the tree as if he were Usain Bolt sprinting down a track. Temi gawked. There was no way she could duplicate that feat; he hadn't even put his sword away for the climb.

More animals were gathering in the shadows, spreading out to surround them. Jakatra must be mistaken. They were definitely hunting with pack instincts. And they were getting closer.

She stuck her sword into the scabbard hanging across her back and slid her hands over the rough bark. When the blade disappeared into its home, its glow quenched, the darkness left behind filled her with as much fear as those howls did. She reached up, gripping the trunk and jumped, trying to dig her boots into the bark. They skidded down several inches. Panic rose in her breast, along with the realization that she might not be able to do this, that she hadn't climbed enough trees as a child.

A high-pitched yowl erupted from the brush not twenty feet away. Sheer adrenaline changed Temi's mind—she *could* do this—and propelled her upward. Her shoes skidded again. She cursed, hugged the tree for all she was worth, and kicked them off. She made much better progress in socks. But was it enough? Heavy paws trod on the undergrowth around the trunk. Snarls and slavering sounds filled her ears.

"Look out," Jakatra yelled from above.

Temi dug in with her feet, left the fingers of one hand wedged between two scales in the bark, and slid the sword out with the other hand. Light splashed the side of the tree and illuminated part of the ground, as well as the black feline-like creature leaping into the air, a paw slashing for her leg.

Temi swatted at it weakly, afraid she would fall from her precarious perch. Luck guided her hand, and she connected with a pointed nose. The creature yowled, and she glimpsed a rack of sharp fangs before it dropped back to the ground. Countless others were swirling around down there.

"Keep climbing, go," came Jakatra's muffled voice from the other side of the trunk.

His unexpected proximity startled her, and that alone was almost enough to upset her balance. He caught her wrist, as if to secure her to the tree. The hilt of his sword was clenched between his teeth. Another feline leaped, but Jakatra let go of Temi and intercepted it with his blade.

She was tempted to stay and help, but he clearly meant to buy her time to climb. And what good would she be if she fell into that snarling mass of animals, anyway? She would only get herself killed. With her eyes on that first branch, she returned to climbing. Instead of putting away the sword and plunging them into darkness again, she tried to use it as an aid. She drove the serrated part into the bark like an anchor, using it to help pull her body up foot by foot. Grunting and straining—and lacking all of Jakatra's agility—she muscled herself up the tree through will and determination. She clasped onto the branch with a great sigh of relief and pulled herself astraddle it, putting her back to the trunk.

Jakatra was right behind her.

"We'll be safe up here?" she asked, squinting into the gloom below. There was a bump halfway up the tree. That couldn't be one of the creatures, could it?

"Safe? No. They can climb."

Temi's heart sank. "Then why...?" Why had they bothered scrambling up to this perch?

"Only one or two can come at us at a time, and we'll have the advantage, the high ground."

Temi grimaced, not sure how advantaged she felt, sitting on a branch. Even as she watched, Jakatra slashed and stabbed at a feline that must have weighed four hundred pounds. It made a tiger look small. The animal hissed and slashed right back at him. Those eerie yips came from the ground, and more creatures started up the tree.

"Turn off the light of your sword so I can see something," Jakatra said, a strange note to his voice. "The glow is disturbing my night vision."

As much as that notion went against her every instinct—surely light could only help her fight these beasts—she commanded the sword to dim, as she had been taught. After its illumination, the night was especially dark, and Temi blinked, willing her eyes to adjust. There were stars up there above the trees, but she hadn't spotted a moon on this world yet.

Clangs and thuds came from below her branch. Temi shifted her weight, trying to find a position where she might help him attack. Standing or crouching on the branch might be best, but then what would she hold onto?

"Look down," Jakatra said.

"I can't see in the dark," she said, though he had to know that by now. She squinted toward the ground, though she didn't expect to pick anything out of the gloom. To her surprise, she spotted a few glowing blue dots moving around the base of the tree. Another was halfway up the trunk. "What the—"

"Command devices," Jakatra said, his voice grim.

"Like the ones the animals that first night were wearing? The animals you said were domesticated?"

"Yes."

"You were controlling those other ones, right? Who's controlling these?"

"I don't know."

"Oh."

8

Temi cut one of the shaggy felines between the eyes, then slashed at the paw gripping the branch she was standing on. The beast let go, tumbling into the darkness below. A startled cry came from it or one of the buddies it landed on. She slumped against the trunk, wiping sweat from her eyes and wishing, for the fiftieth time, she had her water bottle with her.

"I had intended to pit you against a number of different types of animals tonight," Jakatra said from a branch on the other side of the trunk. They had climbed up another ten feet to find separate perches for each of them—and in hopes of deterring the giant cats. That had been two hours ago. They hadn't spoken much; there hadn't been many lulls. "Nothing else will approach while the *saru* are here in such alarming numbers."

Temi wouldn't *want* anything else to approach. She was so tired that she no longer cared about being trained, about her knee, about her career, about anything. She wanted to go home. And if that couldn't happen, a glass of cold lemonade would be almost as good.

The cats were milling suspiciously at the base of the tree. She heard them more than she saw them—the silver illumination of her sword didn't reach the ground—but those angry hisses and eerie yowls marked their presence.

"There is little more to be gained from this. You are tired and the creatures are relentless." Jakatra, his angular face silhouetted by the glow of her sword, gazed toward the starry sky above, then at the nearby trees.

"*You're* not tired?" Temi asked. He never seemed to be, but even he had to be worn down by the constant fighting. He was doing as much as she and with a sword that didn't have nearly as much bite.

"I am no longer satisfied by this situation."

That was probably the closest he would come to admitting weariness. "How many hours until Eleriss comes to get us?" Temi asked.

"Six hours until dawn."

An hour ago, Temi would have stifled a groan, lest he think her complaining. Now, she didn't bother to hide the heartfelt noise of frustration and distress. She hadn't been injured yet, beyond scrapes and bruises, but her back ached from bending and fighting, and she had lost the alertness that had kept her movements crisp in the first few fights. A numb exhaustion was creeping into her body now.

A spitting hiss came from below. One of the creatures was climbing again. Temi straightened, keeping one hand on the trunk and the other on the sword. Her branch was not very wide. If at any point she slipped, the exercise—and her life—would be over.

"When Eleriss comes," Jakatra said, "I will suggest he takes you to a portal."

"To return home?" The notion renewed her flagging energy. Even if Prescott was a long way from the home where she had grown up, Simon and Delia were there, and they would know where to find a lemonade. And their irreverent quips would be welcome after this week of relentless training. "Have I learned enough?"

"Someone is trying to kill you tonight. It is no longer safe for you here."

"How do you know someone's not trying to kill *you*?" she asked lightly, though the implication that she *hadn't* learned enough stung. What had she expected? To become a master sword fighter in less than a week? It had taken her more than ten years to start winning tennis tournaments at the highest level. Besides, she hadn't even wanted to become a sword fighter and a monster slayer, right? She had wanted to fail, to be released from this commitment. That had been the plan anyway. Somewhere along the way, things had changed. Funny how her desire to show Jakatra that she was capable, that she was a worthy student, had turned into an acceptance of her fate.

"It's possible but unlikely," he said. "Murder is uncommon among our people."

"A rule that doesn't extend to humans?"

The creature had climbed close enough to their branches that they had to stop their conversation to deal with it. The animals always came up on her side of the tree, a fact she hadn't missed. She lowered herself to a crouch, the sword raised for a swing. At the same time, Jakatra leaned around the trunk from his own branch.

The cat hissed at him, then sprinted up the side of the tree toward Temi. Her heart tried to jump out of her throat, but this was the fourth or fifth time one of the cats had done this, and she kept her calm, merely meeting it with a slash to the face. Jakatra had more of a stabbing blade than a slicing one, and he rammed the point into its side as it tried to fly past, to make it to Temi's branch. Her weapon cut into the creature's pointed maw, the magic or whatever gave it its power, guiding it deep. The animal screeched, but flung itself upward anyway, its claws raking at her leg.

She stumbled to the side, slashing again and putting her back to the tree. Her heel slipped off the branch, and she almost pitched over the side and fumbled the sword.

Losing *it* would be almost as bad as losing herself over the edge.

With a twist and a wild flinging of her arms, she regained her grip on the hilt, as well as her balance on the branch, but the creature had the time it needed to climb up in front of her. It looked all too comfortable on the narrow perch. It bunched its legs and sprang. There was no way to dodge. With her back to the tree, she lifted a leg to her chest and kicked outward, her heel taking the feline in the face. At the same time, Jakatra swung onto her branch out of nowhere—from above, she thought—landing in a crouch behind the creature. He stabbed it in the back and heaved it sideways, somehow maintaining his own balance on the narrow branch.

The cat fell away, but his sword, embedded deeply in its flesh, didn't come out without a hitch. Temi, her back still against the tree, reached out and grabbed his shoulder to keep him from tumbling after the animal. With his agility, he probably wouldn't have fallen anyway, but he gave her a nod when he straightened up, his sword still in his hand, the creature down among its buddies again. Hopefully dead. A fall of thirty feet *should* kill an animal, shouldn't it? Temi and Jakatra had landed killing blows on some of them, but the milling pack down there never seemed to grow smaller.

"As I was about to say," Jakatra said, "I don't know how the laws would relate to killing humans. Eleriss and I may be the only ones who have interacted with your kind in recent generations. It is likely my people would regard you as a trespasser. Some would evict you through the nearest portal. Others might take more drastic measures." He tilted his chin toward the prowling predators. "I do not think anyone would be punished for slaying a human, not if it happened here. But this method of sending predators... It suggests someone doesn't want to be caught. They must know I'm here as well. I suppose if I were to die out here with you, Eleriss would only be able to report my death as a hunting accident. Perhaps because I am helping you, I am now a target as well."

He didn't sound happy about that. Of course not. He hadn't wanted to help her in the first place.

"These portals," Temi said, "is there any way we could escape to one now?"

"They must be... created—that is not the correct word, but I do not know another in your language—with the... portal opener."

Temi was sure it was all far more sophisticated than someone rolling up to a house and tapping a remote control to open a garage door, but that was what came to mind.

"Eleriss has the device," Jakatra added.

"Of course he does."

Jakatra didn't reply. She expected him to return to his branch, but he remained on hers, standing a couple of feet away, his sword in hand, a silent guardian. She wasn't sure when he had turned from teacher to protector, but he must think she needed protecting now. She hoped that was a reflection of the odds they faced rather than of her ability to handle herself. Fighting on the ground would seem a breeze after this.

"It is possible I erred in seeking out this isolated scenario," Jakatra said.

"Oh?" She couldn't remember him ever admitting to an error.

He gazed toward the dark forest. "When Eleriss gave me this task, I objected to teaching you, to teaching any human."

"Yes, you made that clear."

"You have been..."

Temi arched her brows.

"A good student," he finished.

The compliment surprised her into speechlessness, and she could only gape at him.

"I do not think that killing the *jibtab* will make any difference or change the fate of your world, but I will concede that you are worthy of carrying that sword."

Strange that it felt good to receive praise for a skill she had never wanted to acquire. "Thank you."

"Now I see why they've been quiet," Jakatra said after a few moments.

"Why?"

"They're climbing up that tree." He pointed to another stout trunk about fifteen meters away. "They'll be able to leap down on us from there."

"Great."

A light appeared in the distance, something that reminded her of a headlamp. It was up in the air, a little higher than their branch, and it was coming their way. Jakatra, focused on the felines climbing the tree behind them, didn't seem to have noticed.

"Any chance that's Eleriss?" Temi asked. "Coming early?"

"That is not his truck."

Temi thought about pointing out that the word hovercraft might be more appropriate for their flying vehicles, but it hardly seemed important just then. "Any chance it's someone else coming to help?"

"A chance." Jakatra turned, putting his back to her as he faced the light—it was getting closer. Whoever was flying the craft knew exactly where he was going. "Stay behind me," he added.

Given that she was standing on a branch, Temi couldn't imagine where else she would go, but was happy to follow the order.

The top of the hovercraft was open, and she thought she could pick out a couple of heads in there, but its headlight didn't do anything to illuminate the people riding inside. If they had weapons, she couldn't tell.

She expected the craft to fly closer, but it stopped,

the powerful yellow beam of its headlight sweeping back and forth, searching the trees. Searching for them. The light brushed the snarling felines below—Temi tensed, because a new one was climbing the tree—but it didn't stop there. The beam traveled up the trunk to shine in her and Jakatra's eyes. He lowered into a deep crouch, ready to spring. But where? Thirty feet to the ground? Into the maws of those giant cats?

As if he knew what she was wondering, he looked up, his gaze lingering on a higher branch for a long moment. The sturdy tree would support their weight if they climbed higher, but Temi didn't see how that would help them against a flying car.

The light dropped, and the craft spun in the air, turning its backend toward them. It soared away, and soon the trees hid it from view, though its light was still visible as the craft moved about in the forest. Was it looking for something further? Maybe it was someone out there hunting for mushrooms, someone who wanted nothing to do with the cats or Jakatra and Temi. Of course, if that were the case, she would have expected the people to help, to try and drive the creatures away.

"The appearance of the technology did not scare the *saru* away," Jakatra observed.

"Because these ones are controlled by those glowing dots?" Temi asked.

"Likely." He seemed to have something else on his mind—other suspicions—but that was all he said.

The scrape of claws sinking into bark reminded Temi that they still had other problems. Jakatra moved farther out on the branch, so they could both attack at once. With two swords slashing toward it, they knocked the cat free before it found its way to their level. These small triumphs no longer inspired Temi, not when more creatures would soon start up to take its place.

Jakatra's nose wrinkled, and he faced in the direction

of the hovercraft again. The headlight had disappeared—or wasn't visible from their position—but a new light had appeared, this one orange and flickering.

"Fire?" Temi hooked her arm around the trunk and leaned out for a better view. Her stomach sank. A *lot* of fire. Flames were licking up the side of a tree about a hundred meters away.

"Fire," Jakatra agreed grimly.

9

A NORMAL FOREST FIRE THAT size wouldn't spread quickly and might burn over there all night without bothering them, but Temi had a feeling this wasn't a normal fire. The hovercraft wasn't anywhere in sight, but it was too much of a coincidence to believe flames had randomly started up right after it left. It wasn't even dry here, not like in the forests of her New Mexico homeland.

Jakatra pointed to the right of where Temi had been looking. Another fire was burning in the undergrowth over there. At the base of the tree, the creatures voices changed, concern in their unearthly yips for the first time. They turned, their furry snouts pointing toward the flames. Damn, there was a third spot fire now.

"Is it just me," she said, "or are your people lighting those fires in a circle? To make *sure* we can't escape?"

"This is not logical behavior," Jakatra said. "If they wanted you, or for some reason wanted me, they could shoot from afar with a projectile weapon. To deliberately burn the forest is strange behavior for one of my people."

"Maybe a human got through," she said. It was a joke, or sarcasm at the least, but he answered seriously.

"It was ensured centuries ago that none of the portal keys remained in your world. Unless someone else brought a human here, one could not be present."

"Fires are good for hiding evidence, they say. Maybe someone wants to kill us without being obvious about it." Temi shifted her weight, trying to figure out how they could escape without jumping into the jaws of death down below. Those creatures shouldn't want to stick around for a wildfire, either, but who knew what those blue dots were commanding them to do? None of them had left yet.

"Possibly. That would be in line with the animal attacks." Jakatra faced the trunk and pointed up. "If they seek to surround us with fire, then we must leave first."

"*That* way?" Temi also pointed up.

"I believe that if we go out on that branch approximately twenty feet up, we can make our way to the next tree, and then the next. After that, we'll reassess our route."

Temi stared at the orange flames dancing on the ground, already climbing numerous trees. The scent of smoke had reached her nose now. At least Jakatra wanted to go in the opposite direction from the flames, but she wasn't a squirrel and those branches up there were thin. She and Jakatra were already more than thirty feet off the ground.

"You are capable of this feat," Jakatra said. "Sansolu said so."

"Who?"

"Your healer." Jakatra waved at her knee as he stepped past her. Without brushing her, he leapt and caught the side of the tree, his dexterous fingers easily finding holds in the cracks between plates of bark. "He said you would now be capable of swinging through the trees." He paused, his head tilting in consideration. "In reflection, this may have been an insult in regard to the simian origins of humans."

Temi snorted. "I'll bet."

Jakatra was already climbing, so she sheathed the sword and did her best to follow. The flames had already grown to the point that they illuminated the forest so that she could see without the silvery glow. A fact that was less comforting than one might imagine. "What did elves evolve from?"

"Elves? Ah, yes, that is your word for us."

"I forgot your word." Temi grimaced as her foot slipped on the bark. She should probably be concentrating on climbing.

"We also share origins with a tree-dwelling species, but they were more elegant than your simian cousins."

"Were they snootier and more arrogant than our simian cousins too?"

Jakatra paused to look down at her, the flames of the fire reflected in his violet eyes. She expected a haughty sniff, but he actually seemed to be considering the question.

"The modern ones *do* seem to believe themselves superior to the other wilderness denizens," he said.

"Imagine that."

Temi was almost to the branch Jakatra had pointed to from below. A few more feet, and she could pull herself up to a safe spot. Too bad he wouldn't let her stay there long.

Bark crumbled beneath her fingers, and she lunged for the branch with her other hand. She grasped it at the same time as the bark gave way, splinters digging beneath her nails as wood fell. For a second, she hung there by one hand, wondering how many more times her heart would try to leap out of her chest before it succeeded.

Jakatra, already standing on the branch, looked down at her. Doubtlessly wondering what was taking so long. Temi swung up her other hand and hauled herself onto the slender branch. As soon as her feet were on it, Jakatra jogged along its length, the wood shivering beneath his steps, and leaped a couple of feet, landing on an equally slender limb stretching across from the next tree. He trotted out of the way, then stopped to wait again.

Temi wiped sweat out of her eyes, spread her arms for balance, and tightrope-walked after him. She wished for some of the gripping skills of those simian cousins. Her shoes lay at the bottom of the tree, and she had flung her socks down at some point, as well, so she tried to use her toes, but mostly she relied on her balance, inching farther and farther. The branch trembled, growing narrower as she moved along it. The snaps and cracks of the fire reached her ears, adding pressure to the situation. As if the yips and whines coming from the base of the tree weren't enough. Temi kept hoping the animals would take off, but a handful of them were following her progress from the ground, their snouts tilting upward as if she were the only food they had seen in months.

"You will find it easier with more momentum," Jakatra said when she stopped at the point where he had crossed.

"Good to know," Temi said and very carefully made the jump. She bent her knees and spread her arms, catching her balance on the new branch. "Next," she said when she got over the relief of making it.

Jakatra led her to the trunk, then out onto a branch on the other side. Temi did her best to keep up, all too aware of how quickly that fire was spreading.

A whine like that of a mosquito, but louder, sounded, and one of the branches above her snapped. It fell, nearly dropping onto her head. She batted it aside with her arm, but it upset her balance, leaving her flailing for her life once again.

"What was *that*?" she blurted when she had regained her balance.

"A projectile weapon not unlike your firearms." Jakatra pointed into the air above the fire. The hovercraft was back, its beam probing the trees again, the smoke making the light hazy, surreal. This whole damned experience was surreal. "Hurry." He ran along the branch as he spoke, jumping onto the next one.

"Hurry *where*?" Temi growled, though she raced after him as quickly as she dared. She grudgingly admitted that he had been right, that it was easier when she went faster instead of checking her balance every inch of the way. But it hardly mattered. The cats were guarding the ground, whoever had the gun was guarding the air, and the fire was coming from the side. Where could they possibly flee to? "We're going to have to confront... somebody."

The animals, the people, she didn't know which confrontation they would be more likely to survive, but they were targets at the moment.

Another whining weapon fired, blasting into the side of a trunk. Bark flew everywhere, this time battering Jakatra. So, he was as much of a target as she. Later, Temi might find that interesting, but right now, she was too busy trying not to fall off the branches. She lunged behind a trunk, expecting to have to climb to another branch, but Jakatra was waiting there, the bulk of the tree hiding them from the hovercraft.

He gripped her arm. "You are correct. I will confront my people. You continue in the trees. Get as far as you can. Make sure you're out of the fire's path." He pointed in a direction, though how he could tell which way the fire would turn, she couldn't guess. "Don't go down unless you're certain the animals have given up the chase. Even then, stay near the trees. Eleriss will find you eventually."

She imagined him snoozing in a bed—or a funky hammock—back in a city somewhere. "At dawn?"

"No later than that. He is punctual." Jakatra shifted his weight to go back the way they had come.

"Wait, are you sure you don't want help with them?" She surprised herself with the offer. It wasn't her fight—they had brought her here, after all—but he might need help. And she didn't want to lose someone who had spent the night keeping an eye out for her.

"They shouldn't be your concern. You must return to your world with your weapon to protect your people." Jakatra pointed to her sword scabbard. "And I believe you will do so."

"But..." Temi stretched out a hand toward him, struggling to articulate what she wanted to say. "I don't want to lose another coach."

"I will see that this is not the case." Jakatra gave her a solemn nod, then took off across the branches, maneuvering along them more easily than she would ever be able to.

More whining shots fired, and she winced, dreading the idea of him being killed. Especially if there was a way it would be her fault again. They may have brought her here, but they were doing it to help her world. And she had agreed to come, whatever her motivations had been. She was the reason the forest was burning.

Temi brushed her damp eyes. They were tears of frustration, she told herself, nothing more, nothing... weaker. Then she took off in the opposite direction, toward the dark forest night, putting the burning trees at her back.

She picked a route through the branches for minutes that felt like hours. It was hard to tell. Smoke filled the dark sky, and she couldn't see the fire any more, nor the hovercraft. It was all she could do to concentrate on the trees, on running along the branches with legs and arms that grew ever wearier. Growls, yips, and yowls sounded from the ground from time to time. She didn't know if they belonged to those cats or simply to creatures fleeing the fire, but she was afraid to drop to the forest floor to find out. So long as the latticework of branches provided a path, she would follow it. Ash coated her tongue, and she was so thirsty, her lips had cracked. Her skin felt flushed and fevered, and she didn't know how much farther she could go.

When a light appeared ahead of her, Temi was so numb that it didn't register to her brain at first. As soon as it did, she halted, grabbing a trunk with hands scraped so raw they were bleeding. It wasn't fire; it was a headlamp again. The hovercraft. Jakatra must not have caught up with it. Or maybe there was more than one.

She leaned her temple against the rough bark, tired of running, tired of all of this.

The beam of light swept through the haze toward her. She tried to scoot behind the trunk, to hide herself. She gripped the hilt of her sword, but didn't draw it. She was too tired to command the blade not to glow and didn't want it giving her away.

The hovercraft drifted closer through the smoke.

"Artemis?"

She lifted her head. Was that...? "Eleriss?"

"Yes. I am here. We must return you to your home."

Temi had never heard words that sounded so sweet, but it took a while before she could force her arm to release its death grip on the tree trunk. Not until Eleriss's pointed ears and blue eyes came into view did her grip relax.

He pulled up, his craft hovering below the branch she stood upon. "Jump in, please. Time is a concern."

Temi swung down into the seat beside him, banging her feet on her tennis bag. Eleriss must have guessed this would be her last night and she would have to leave. Had he also guessed this night of hunting could turn into something much different than she had envisioned? That the hunters would become the hunted?

Questions for another time. She sank back into the seat. She was so relieved to be sitting in something solid—as solid as a chair in a floating car could be—that she almost cried. But smoke still clogged the air, stinging her eyes and reminding her that they weren't free of danger.

"Jakatra, have you seen him? He went back to confront the..." She waved vaguely in the direction she thought the fire had started, though she had lost track of much up in the trees.

"I will return for him, but I must send you home first." Eleriss pressed his palm against a soft gel pad, pushing with his fingers, and the hovercraft pulled away from the tree. It zipped through the smoke, heading away from Jakatra instead of toward him.

Temi tried not to feel like she had left another coach to die, but the bleakness threatened to overwhelm her.

"As soon as we reach a clear area, I'll open a portal," Eleriss said.

"Will you be coming back? At some point? I'd like to hear about... if Jakatra made it."

Eleriss gave her that polite smile of his. "Jakatra is extremely capable. I highly doubt a fire or a couple of our own people could trouble him overmuch."

Temi wasn't sure whether to believe him or not. "I feel cowardly running away from something that is... at least partially my fault, or a result of my being here anyway."

The hovercraft had come into clear air, air that seemed a touch lighter, promising dawn's approach, and Eleriss brought it to a stop and faced her in his seat. "You will not be running away from something. You will be running toward something. Another *jibtab* has appeared in your world. Your comrades need your help."

Temi let her chin droop to her chest. If Simon and Delia would be in trouble soon, she had to go back to help them, but she struggled to walk away from this... unfinished business. For all she knew, neither Eleriss nor Jakatra nor anyone else would ever return to her world, not now that they had retrieved the sword and trained a human to use it.

"You will go to them and help fight it, yes?" Eleriss asked, his blue eyes scrutinizing her.

She wondered if he had known about her thoughts from the week before, her notion that she might take the healed knee and return to the tennis world. Forget the *jibtab* and being Earth's warrior. But that would have been if she had failed the training, if they had been forced to look for someone else. Thanks to Jakatra, she hadn't. She didn't know what the next *jibtab* would look like, but she had practice fighting terrifying predators now. He'd said she was competent. And that had pleased her, even if it condemned her to... whatever fate awaited her back home.

"Triumph and disaster," she muttered.

"Pardon?" Eleriss asked.

"Yes, I will fight them."

"Good." Eleriss hopped out of the vehicle and pulled a device out of his pocket. He pressed it, and the blue portal flared to life, as it had a week ago, on a dark deserted logging road in the mountains of Arizona.

Temi gazed toward the trees, back in the direction they had come from, where smoke hugged the canopy, tendrils bleeding up into the sky.

"It is the middle of your nighttime," Eleriss said, "so I have not placed the portal exit far from the city, but you should go through soon, lest someone else notices it."

"Yes, that would be hard to explain." Temi sighed and started to turn away from the forest, but something stirred the smoke, and she paused.

A tall lean form strode out of the haze, walking soundlessly across the leaf litter and pine needles, the hilt of a sword poking up over his shoulder. The light from the portal shone across Jakatra's features, his face smudged by soot and grime, and marred by more than a few bruises.

"Greetings," Eleriss said. "It is good that you have come to say farewell to your student. She was most reluctant to leave while your fate was unknown."

As tired and numb as she was after the night, Temi found the energy to blush at this statement. It wasn't as if she was some pining lover. She just hadn't wanted to leave without knowing if he lived or died, that was all.

Jakatra gave her a curious look, though he didn't comment on Eleriss's words, instead going straight to business.

Destiny Unchosen

"I caught up with those who were shooting at us. I convinced them to fly away," Jakatra said coolly, a lot left unsaid, Temi was certain. "They were unwilling to speak openly to me, and I was not inclined to interrogate anyone—" he gave Eleriss a long look that Temi couldn't decipher, "—but I construed that Artemis was only part of the problem. That she has that sword is another part. *We* are another part." His eyes narrowed, never leaving Eleriss's face. "People know now that we have been helping humans."

"The sword is a problem?" Eleriss asked, ignoring the other issues. Maybe he had already known about them. "But it came from Earth, where it had been buried for centuries. Why would anyone here care about it or even know of its existence?"

"I don't know," Jakatra said.

Eleriss frowned at Temi's scabbard. What would she do if he asked for it back? A week ago, she would have offered it to him freely, but after going through so much with it, she would be reluctant to part with it. "Your friends who like to do the research," he said, "perhaps they can learn more about the weapon. Perhaps it has a history we do not know."

"I'm sure they'll be willing to do that." If they hadn't already. That first night, Simon had taken a few thousand pictures of the sword and scabbard from different angles, with Delia nearby, looking up historical weapons on the Internet.

"You had better join them now." Eleriss cast a nervous glance back toward the woods, maybe wondering if Jakatra had done anything more than buy them a little time.

"I will." Temi hid the sword in her bag and hefted it over her shoulder. Hoping for a hug or a pat on the shoulder from Jakatra was probably too much, but she gave him a nod, like the one he had given her before going off, before stepping up to the portal.

"Don't forget," Jakatra said. "Momentum can solve a lot of problems."

Certain he was talking about more than running across branches, she nodded and said, "I'll remember."

Temi gave them both long looks, then strode through the portal.

THE END

Made in United States
Orlando, FL
05 August 2023